Hanukkah Hearts
Jean C. Joachim

Moonlight Books

Dedication

To David and Steve, who always enjoyed the Hanukkah celebration.

Acknowledgment

T hank you to my editors, Laura, and my proofreader, Renee Waring. A special "thank you" to Vicki Locey, and Roz Lee whose encouragement keeps me on track. Thank you to Roz for suggesting the idea of the Hanukkah Elf. Thank you to the Joachim men, Larry, David & Steve, and the newest member of our family, Pam, for keeping me grounded and believing in me.

Hanukkah Hearts
Copyright © 2019 Jean C. Joachim
Edited by Laura Garland+
Proofreader: Renee Waring
Cover design – Dawne Dominique, Dusk to Dawn designs

PUBLISHER
Moonlight Books

Chapter One

Pushing against the winterish wind as she walked toward the Hudson River, Becky Cohen sniffed the sweet aroma of a wood fire. The scent cut through the frigid December air, reminding her of home. The memory of sitting in front of the fireplace with her family at Hanukkah flashed through her mind. She sighed. Yeah, but not this year. Hanukkah didn't coincide with Christmas on the calendar, so she didn't have time off. She had a ticket to fly back to Milwaukee when the office closed for the holiday.

The bitter cold stung Becky's face as she trudged along 92nd street toward her apartment building. She bowed her head and pulled her wool scarf tighter. The icy air sliced through her clothing, penetrating straight to the bone. The wind off Riverside Drive, more wicked than anything she'd experienced in Milwaukee, howled around her.

Anxious to get back to the small two-bedroom apartment she shared with three other young women, she quickened her steps. Shutting her eyes for a second, she couldn't wipe away the humiliating episode that had occurred moments before.

As she made her way home, she shuddered at the recollection of being caught in tears by the hunky Assistant Production Manager, Sam Golden. At six o'clock, she'd thought everyone had left, so she took a moment to Skype her family on her phone, to share a bit of the first night of Hanukkah via the Internet.

Her brothers, David and Joe, had answered. She'd never forget David's words.

"Hey, Squirt. Listen, Mom took a turn for the worse. Dad took her to the hospital. Hanukkah's been cancelled."

She didn't remember the rest of their conversation. Her mind had blanked after the word "hospital." David didn't have any new details about their mother. Myra Cohen had contracted a bad case of the flu, which turned into pneumonia. Maybe the antibiotic wasn't working or something? Becky couldn't remember because she'd gone straight to panic mode. She'd gotten off quickly and burst into tears. Sobbing into a lone tissue she'd fished from her desk drawer, she started when a deep voice said, "Here." A hand bearing a clean, white handkerchief came into view.

She raised her wet gaze to meet Sam Golden's. His gorgeous green eyes held concern.

"Boyfriend problems?"

She shook her head, trying to pull herself together enough to talk. "No boyfriend. My mother."

"Mother problems?" He raised his eyebrows. "At this age?"

"Sick. She's sick. They've taken her to the hospital."

"Oh, geez. Crap. I'm sorry." He sank down into the chair next to her desk.

She took his offering and hid her face behind it, muttering, "Thank you."

"And on the first night of Hanukkah, too." He shook his head.

"Hanukkah's been cancelled," she said, her words muffled by the cloth.

"Cancelled? I didn't know you could cancel Hanukkah. I'd better call my family." He started to rise.

Despite herself, Becky smiled and put her hand on his arm. "Just for my family."

"I'm sorry. That's so sad."

Fresh tears welled up. "I'd better go." She pushed to her feet. Upon standing, Becky lost her balance. Sam rose, grabbed her, and held her.

"Thank you," she mumbled, her mind muddled, her pulse racing.

His tender embrace unleashed new emotions in her. Unable to stop herself, she cried on his shoulder. He tightened his grip with one arm and stroked her back with his free hand.

"I bet she's gonna be okay."

His warm, reassuring words, and strength soothed her. Her eyes drifted shut. How many times had she dreamt of being in Sam Golden's arms? A hundred? A thousand? Maybe, okay, definitely, but never like this. Her mom's favorite expression echoed in her head. "Get a grip, girl." A few deep breaths helped her regain control and she stepped back.

She wiped her face with his hanky, then gazed up. "I'll wash this and return it."

He waved it away. "Keep it. I have dozens. Probably gonna get more for Hanukkah, too."

She managed a small smile, then tucked his gift into her bag.

"It's late. Let me put you in a cab."

"The subway. I'm saving money to go home at the holiday."

"Oh, okay. I'll walk you."

Together they donned winter coats, scarves, hats, and gloves to brave the brutish December weather.

Becky approached her townhouse-sized apartment building and recalled Sam's kindness. She'd had such a crush on him from the day she started at Homes and Ralph Publishing a year ago.

He stood six feet tall with brown hair and green eyes. Narrow at the waist, he had wide shoulders and a dazzling grin. The second their gazes connected her heart flipped. The heat of his stare penetrated places best ignored during the workday.

Sam was an important manager and rumored to be dating Maryann Donnelley, her boss. That and the fact she was only an editorial assistant put him off-limits. Still, she could dream, right? Sam and Maryann went out to lunch every other week. Occasionally, after hours, he'd disappear into her office and close the door. She wondered what went on in there but had no way to satisfy her curiosity.

At twenty-eight, Becky wasn't some naïve schoolgirl. Or a virgin, either. In fact, her shiny, dark hair, deep chocolate eyes, and curvy figure had attracted boys since sophomore year in high school. She'd had a different boyfriend every year in college, too.

Against her father's wishes, Becky had moved to New York. The noise, the crowds, and the pulse of the City overwhelmed her, though she'd never admit it.

"Why can't you stay here? You have a good job at the Daily Sentinel. New York is expensive and dangerous. You're dating a nice boy, get married. You can move out then."

"I'm not staying here, Dad. Even if I don't leave Milwaukee, I'm getting my own apartment."

"Why? Save money. Live at home."

She snorted. "Yeah, right. I'm twenty-seven. It's way past time."

"If you go to New York, don't come crying to me for airfare to come home when you get homesick. If you're so damn independent, pay for it yourself. In fact, pay for everything yourself. I'm done."

And he'd huffed off, slamming the front door behind him. His lack of support had rattled her. But, after a day or two, her resolve hardened, and she made plans to move to the Big Apple.

A headhunter set her up with several job interviews and Becky had nailed the best one. She landed the job as admin assistant to two acquisitions editors at Homes and Ralph Publishing. She hoped to become an acquisitions editor herself someday. When she was hired at H and P, she'd taken the first step toward living her dream.

Finding a place to live had been a challenge. Once she'd closed the deal on an apartment share, she'd taken her savings, shipped her stuff, and hopped on a plane. Becky had lucked out with her three roommates. While not becoming her best friends, they had a live-and-let-live attitude. After a few months of adjustment, they settled into peaceful co-existence. They went their way and she went hers.

On Friday nights, anyone left dateless chipped in for a pizza or Chinese food. They ate together and watched a movie. Becky had spent far too many Friday nights in the apartment. Often, she wondered what delicious meal her mother was creating for their family Shabbos dinner.

After heading to bakery after bakery, Becky finally found one that still had one loaf of fresh Challah left on a Friday night after work. But without her family, or even Jewish friends to light a candle, say the prayers and share the loaf, it didn't mean much.

Monday was the first night of Hanukkah. After searching store-after-store, Becky had lucked out at Zabar's finding an affordable, tiny menorah, and candles that fit. She'd called her brother.

"So, you're not gonna be here for Hanukkah. We can Skype," Joe had said.

"I don't know how to Skype on my computer."

"It's the same as the phone. I'll walk you through it."

"We could light the lights together then?"

"Right, Squirt."

When she reached the front door, Becky shook the dusting of snow off her shoulders, and entered the warmth of the lobby. After climbing two flights, she unlocked the door. The three women who shared her digs were gobbling down chicken lo mein and watching a movie. They acknowledged her presence for a moment to tell her about the food.

Becky hung up her coat, filled a bowl and went to her room. With her little menorah perched proudly on the windowsill, she could watch the candles burn from her bed. She struck a match and recited the prayers. A lump of emotion closed her throat as loneliness seeped into her bones. No family, no gifts, no laughter. She stared at the bowl of noodles which was no substitute for latkes with home-made applesauce, and her mother's brisket. She sighed and dug into her paltry meal.

Her mind wandered back to the crazy gag gifts she'd exchanged with her family over the years. A chef's apron for her father who never cooked, a Slinky for her older brother, a subscription to Mad Magazine for her mother! Every day, they'd draw a name and give a present to the person on the next night.

Scrambling through crowded stores, searching for just the right gift at the last minute had been a challenge. Maybe their method had been a bit nuts, but humor reigned, bringing the most precious gifts of all; laughter, joy, and love.

When she finished eating, Becky picked up a romance novel and dove into it. She needed to forget her embarrassing encounter with Sam, not to mention the fact her mother may be seriously ill with Becky over eight hundred miles away.

AFTER A DEPRESSING first night of Hanukkah, Becky overslept. She dragged herself into work fifteen minutes late. A package sat on her desk. Damn, that hadn't been there the day before. She didn't know whether to open it or call security. The rectangular box, wrapped in blue and white paper with a blue ribbon and a big bow, intrigued her.

"Open it, please. Open it," pleaded her friend and fellow admin assistant, Joy.

"Come on. We've been staring at it for the last fifteen minutes," added Bridget.

"What if it's a bomb? Will you sweep up my body parts and ship them to my parents?"

"Don't be ridiculous," Joy snapped.

When Becky picked up the package, a card fell out. It read: *Happy Hanukkah, from the Hanukkah Elf.*

"The Hanukkah Elf? What Hanukkah Elf?" Becky asked.

"The Hanukkah Elf? How cool! Is there such a thing?" Joy asked.

"Not as far as I know. This is weird." Becky shook her head.

"What's this?" Sam Golden wandered over. Becky sensed heat in her cheeks at facing him. But he made no mention of the night before. He probably wanted to forget her embarrassing display of emotion as much as she did.

"Someone left this on my desk. I don't know whether to open it or call the bomb squad."

Sam picked up the box and shook it. The young women jumped back.

"Don't!" Becky shrieked.

"Seems okay to me," he said. "Go on. Open it."

Slowly, Becky peeled off the tape and the paper. Inside were candies made of caramel, pecan, and chocolate in the shape of turtles.

"Who sent it?" Joy asked.

"I don't know," Becky replied.

"The Hanukkah Elf!" Bridget laughed.

"Ooh, I love it! A secret admirer." Joy clasped her hands together in front of her chest and sighed.

"He must know I like to feed the turtles in Central Park." Becky offered the sweets to her friends. Sam raised his hand.

"No thanks."

"Turtles," Becky mused, biting into a piece.

After wiping the chocolate off her hands, Becky turned on her computer and opened her email. A month ago, she'd been promoted to senior administrative assistant at Homes and Ralph Publishing. Now her inbox overflowed with assignments and requests from additional acquisitions editors. Becky discovered two new manuscripts waiting for her to read and evaluate.

She set about her work, taking only one coffee break. The machine was empty, so she loaded it up and hit "brew". While she waited, she peeked into Sam's office. He had his door open and held the phone to his ear.

Sam had sexy hair that flopped over his forehead like the actor, Adrian Brody. She longed to comb it back with her fingers. As the aroma of the java wafted her way, she sighed. Being management and dating an editor put Sam in the "hands-off" category.

She didn't like her boss, Maryann Donnelley. Recalling Maryann's recent overblown announcement about her vacation plans to the staff, Becky shifted in her seat.

"I'm going skiing before the holiday. Staying at Evan Watson's place. You know, Evan, the movie director who won the Oscar last year?"

The support staff made fun of Maryann's incessant name-dropping behind her back. In the company cafeteria downstairs, Becky had entertained her friends with an imitation.

"Well, I'm going skiing in Switzerland on the best Alp in the world. And I'm staying at God's house. You know the biggest chalet in the country in the world! If I play my cards right, I might just give birth to another Messiah."

Her friends cracked up. When she looked up and saw Sam watching, she lowered her voice. He shook his head briefly but shot her a smile as he headed for the elevator. She had wanted to die. He'd heard the whole thing. Mortified she'd made fun of his girlfriend, she'd avoided him for a week, until his charisma drew her like iron to a magnet.

When the coffeemaker finished, she poured herself a cup and raised the pot where Sam could see it. Still on the phone, he nodded and held up his mug. She strolled over and filled it, then returned to the machine. Waiting for her was Trevor Gorman, best-selling author of detective stories and every woman's orgasmic dream—except hers.

"How about a refill for me?" He crept up behind her. She complied, then set down the pot. "Don't go. Free for lunch?" He stepped closer invading Becky's space. She moved away. His obvious attempts to get her into bed made her skin crawl.

"Can't today. Sorry. On bad weather days, I bring my lunch." Becky grabbed her coffee and made a beeline for her desk. Not one to give up the chase easily, Trevor ambled over. He leaned against it and chattered to her about himself.

"I'm sorry, but if I don't get this letter done, I'll get yelled at. Please excuse me, Trevor, but I have to work."

"Sure, sure. I get it. Don't want to get you fired or anything. How'd you like that little Hanukkah gift?" Becky's head snapped up. Could Trevor be the Hanukkah Elf? She bit her lip. Trevor, the Adonis in love with himself, wouldn't give a gift to a lowly admin assistant, would he?

Homes and Ralph had a spare office set up for their best-selling authors to use. This month, Trevor held the key. He ambled back inside, grinned at her, and shut the door.

Joy leaned over the partition between their cubicles. "Maybe he's the Hanukkah Elf?"

"God forbid." Becky turned her attention back to her work. But the idea stayed with her.

Shortly before noon, she glanced out the window at the snow falling gently, muffling the sounds of the city, and grinned. Sam always ate in the cafeteria on bad weather days. Rain, snow, and sleet kept him from business lunches. At twelve sharp, Becky retrieved her brown bag from the refrigerator and headed downstairs. She managed to get there five minutes before he showed up.

After purchasing his food, Sam rounded the corner and stopped at her table.

"Mind if I join you?"

"Not at all," Becky tried to dial down her smile from a thousand watts to five hundred.

He placed his tray down then sat. "Figured out who sent you the candy yet?"

She shook her head. "Nope. The girls think Trevor's the Hanukkah Elf."

"Might be. He seems to be hound-dogging you."

"That's not new."

"Really?" Sam quirked an eyebrow as he laid a napkin on his lap.

"He's barking up the wrong tree with me. Mister hound dog is going to find himself neutered, if he doesn't back off."

Sam laughed.

"I mean it. I'll report him to Mr. Ralph if I have to."

"Trevor's one of our biggest authors. I hear his agent is negotiating for a movie deal."

"A movie?"

"Yep. And if it gets released, we'll have to send our plant into overdrive to keep up with the demand for his books."

"That's good for the company, right? But maybe not the best time to report him?" She frowned.

"The buck always comes first. I'll speak to him."

"Thanks. He needs to take 'no' for an answer." She raised her glass of juice to her lips.

"How are you doing?" He narrowed his eyes.

"Fine." She cast her gaze to her food. Damn, he hadn't forgotten.

"About Hanukkah. Your mom."

"Yeah. Well, Mom's still in the hospital. And Hanukkah's still cancelled."

"How do you feel?"

"Crummy. I hate that she's sick. Hate not being able to be there to help out. I hate having no holiday. It sucks." Emotion gripped Becky. She put down her sandwich. Sam took her hand and squeezed it. "I'm sorry."

"I feel guilty about the presents thing. I know I shouldn't expect anything, but we've done it for so many years. Last night I lit the first candle by myself. I felt empty."

"Is your mom going to be okay?"

"I don't know. It's touch-and-go. Dad says she has a good chance. And she's a fighter. So I'm hopeful."

"Maybe tonight'll be better. At least you got a present today."

"The candy? Probably Joy or Bridget. A joke or something. Stringing me along, making me wonder who it is so I won't think about the holiday or Mom."

"Really?" He raised his eyebrows.

"Yeah. It's either one of them, or that sleazebag, Trevor Gorman. Probably one of the girls."

"You lit the lights by yourself?" He took a forkful of meatloaf.

She nodded. "My roommates aren't Jewish. They were curious last year, but the novelty's worn off. I like to keep up the tradition, even if it's just me. What about you?"

"On the weekend, I'll go to my brother's place. He's married. Got a couple of kids. Hanukkah is great with kids. They can hardly wait."

"I remember how it used to be. I have two older brothers. We'd press our noses against the picture window, waiting for Dad."

"Me, too. I can still feel the butterflies in my stomach as he walked through the door and my mother struck the first match."

Becky smiled. "Innocent times. Now I'm so far away."

"Where does your family live?" Sam speared a string bean with his fork.

"In Milwaukee. I'm the only one to fly the coop. My father didn't want me to come to New York. But the publishing business is here. If I wanted to be an editor—which I do—I knew I'd have to be in New York. What brings you to the Big Apple?"

"I'm from New Jersey. Northern Jersey. My parents own a restaurant there. I'm in the city five days then two at the plant, about twenty miles from their place."

"Nice. Just a brother or do you have other siblings, too?"

"Two sisters. One older, one younger. The baby's in the city now, but her husband is looking for a job somewhere they can afford a house and a backyard."

"So it'll be just you here?"

"My older sister's here, too." He scooped up some potatoes. Becky glanced at his plate.

"Is that stuff any good?"

"It's not exactly home cooking. But it'll do. On a bad weather day, hot food works."

She licked her lips. What she wouldn't give for a hot, home-cooked meal. But her budget didn't allow for cafeteria hot food, just a drink and maybe a dessert occasionally. Otherwise, she brought her lunch. A sandwich—often, peanut butter and jelly—cheapest eats on the planet.

When his gaze met hers, she realized she'd been staring at his food. She peeled her banana.

"You bring lunch every day. Don't you get tired of it?"

"I get tired of a lot of things, but I have to do them anyway."

"Budget?"

She nodded.

"Do you think your mystery person will give you something tomorrow, too?"

She shook her head. "I can count on the girls for one good deed, but I don't think I should push my luck."

Sam checked his watch and pushed back his chair. "Time to get back."

"Oh. Yes. Me, too."

Together they walked to the elevator. Curious to learn everything about publishing, Becky peppered Sam with questions about book production. When others pushed in next to them, they were squeezed together. She got a whiff of his aftershave. Smooth, very smooth, with a touch of sweetness. She took a couple of deep breaths and sighed.

"You okay?" he asked.

"Fine." Lowering her gaze, she hoped to hide her burning cheeks.

They got off on the seventh floor. "See ya," he said, heading for his office.

Becky glanced at his back as he walked away. His suit jacket pulled just a tiny bit across his broad shoulders. Even his walk exuded power. A few female heads turned as he sauntered by. The man had magnetism, and, obviously, she wasn't the only one to feel it.

She enjoyed talking to Sam. He seemed to show an interest in her drab little life and didn't come on to her. Not that she would have rejected him, but it showed respect. He had one quality often rare in a man—he was a good listener. His attention had lifted her spirits on such a cold, wet, miserable day. She smiled to herself. Only Sam Golden made a snowy, damp day sing.

Chapter Two

The next morning, Becky pulled on her heavy-duty boots for the second day in a row. Last night, three inches of snow had accumulated. She tromped through the slippery mess to her office, arriving early. The gray, windy day stole her good mood, leaving her feeling mopey and sorry for herself. She stomped off the snow and headed for her cubicle. Stopping to take off her coat, she almost sat before she saw the tiny shopping bag on her chair.

It was a shiny, metallic pink—her favorite color. Once again, fear filled her as she gazed at the gift. She picked up a pen and gingerly used it to pull open the top, to see what was inside without disturbing the package. No luck.

"I'm going to hang up my coat, get coffee, and maybe it will be gone when I return."

Becky added milk to her beverage and returned to her desk. In her absence, the rest of the staff had gathered. The gift still sat proudly taking possession of her chair. A card dangled off the bag's handle.

Joy whipped around the partition and stopped. "Another present?"

"I don't know."

Trevor Gorman ambled over. "I heard about this yesterday. What's in there?"

"Don't you know?" Joy asked in a flirty voice. "I thought you were her Hanukkah Elf."

Trevor's face colored. "Me? Uh. Well. You never know."

His weak denial convinced Becky he'd lied. Damn, it was him!

"I've got a meeting," he said, disappearing down the hall.

"Oh my God. Another present?" Bridget was joined by a woman from accounting and Sam's secretary.

The women clustered around. "Open it. Open it!"

Becky couldn't resist. If it came from Trevor, it couldn't be a bomb because he wasn't smart enough to make one. Besides, he wouldn't blow her up until he'd slept with her. So, she was safe. She picked up the bag by the handles and reached inside, her fingers brushed against something soft. She pulled it out.

Damn! A pug Beany Baby! A small, soft, stuffed pug dog, just like Trixie and Norton, her parents' real-life pugs. Her eyes watered at the thought of the beloved dogs she hadn't seen in ages.

"A pug! How adorable!" Bridget said, snatching the gift. She and Joy cooed over it.

"What's all the fuss?" Maryann asked.

The young women murmured something and scattered like roaches in harsh light.

"Hmm. Stuffed animals in the office? Not professional, Rebecca."

Becky opened a drawer and placed the gift inside.

"Better," Maryann said. "Please come in after my meeting with Trevor. I have a few things for you. Have you finished that new manuscript by Gordon Albright?"

"Not yet."

"What are you waiting for. I need your evaluation by end of day, latest!" The tall, thin woman turned on her four-inch heels and strode away.

"So romantic! Just like from a book. An anonymous lover," crooned Joy, over the partition.

"Whoever he is, he knows I like turtles and pugs. The live ones, I mean."

"Guess he does. Do you think it's Trevor?" Joy asked.

"I think it's you," Becky said, hiding a smile.

"Me?" Joy's mouth fell open.

"Yeah. It's crazy nice, like something you'd do."

"Wish I could take credit. But it wasn't me. I guess Trevor must have a nice side," Joy said.

"We've never seen it," Bridget added.

"We haven't seen it because it doesn't exist." Becky pulled up the manuscript Maryann had referenced. "I've gotta finish this."

Joy returned to her cubicle. Becky leaned back in her chair, resting her feet on her trash can, and clamped a pen between her teeth as she read. This was her favorite part of the job, reading submissions. She had to wade through a lot of crappy, wannabe books, but when she found a good one, electricity shot through her.

Acquisitions was the first step toward creating a bestseller and a famous author. Her interest piqued. Maybe this book would be the one to rocket its writer into fame and fortune and launch her right into the promotion of her dreams.

Still running behind at noon, Becky ate at her desk and kept reading. Truth be told, she'd gotten so engrossed in the story, she didn't want to put it down, even to take a chance that Sam would be in the cafeteria.

The romantic adventure had a protagonist every woman fantasized about: handsome, brave, and funny. She pictured the character of Washington Smith as another Indiana Jones. Inhaling her food while her eyes flew across page after page, she finished eating in twenty minutes.

"Got that evaluation yet?" Maryann popped her head out of her office.

"Almost."

"How's it look?"

"Like a blockbuster."

BECKY STAYED UNTIL six thirty to finish writing her evaluation of the adventure book. A quick glance outside told her it had stopped snowing. She bundled into her down jacket and shoved a hat down over her brown curls. Exhaustion seeped through her. She yawned as she pushed through the door.

The frigid air jarred her awake as she headed for the subway and prayed it wouldn't be crowded. She caught the train at 14th Street and rode it all the way to 96th.

Fortunately, it was late, and she snagged a seat. The ride seemed to take forever if you had to stand. Dipping her hand into her purse, she closed her fingers around the squishy stuffed pug. The covering was soft and velvety, reminding her of Trixie's fur. Becky sighed. How she'd love a snuggle with her pugs. The little cloth companion would have to do.

When she reached the apartment, there was enough Chinese food leftover to serve as dinner. Her roommates watched *Serendipity*, with John Cusack. Becky padded into her room and put candles in her menorah. Taking out her pug, she rested it up against the windowsill as she lit the lights and said the prayer. Watching the small flames, she Skyped her family. Joe, her oldest brother, answered.

"How's Mom?" Becky asked.

"About the same. No change, yet. But the doctor is hopeful."

Becky's shoulders sagged. "Oh."

"But look who's here!"

A bark greeted her ears as her brother picked up both pugs and held them close to the phone. Norton mushed his face right up against the device. All Becky could see was something dark, and then wetness smeared across the screen. She laughed in spite of the dispiriting news.

In the background, she heard, "No, Trixie, stop. Come on Norton. Get down, guys. Down." The picture wobbled, then focused on a pug sporting a wide grin. Norton had always been a ham. Joe put down Trixie while managing to keep the male pug from falling.

"Best laugh all day, Joe."

"Figured they'd cheer you up."

"You're coming home soon, right?" David asked.

"Yeah. Sunday. Early. You'd better be there."

"We will," Joe said.

She heard the sound of the doorbell in the background.

"Pizza's here," David announced.

"Haven't either of you learned to cook?" Becky cocked an eyebrow.

"Nope. And it's not looking like that's happening anytime soon. Gotta go, squirt, before David eats it all. Love you, Beck." After a few barks, the screen went dark.

Becky changed into a nightgown and crawled into bed. She took the stuffed pug with her and switched off the light. Touching the little critter, she recalled Norton and Trixie. Remembering some of their antics put a smile on her face. The rescue dogs were eight years old. Becky had brought them home from college on vacation.

When she entered the house with the dogs, her parents had gone ballistic. Reiterating a thousand times how she couldn't keep them, her folks fell under the pugs' magic spell. By the end of vacation, her mother had surprised her.

"I hope you hadn't planned on taking Trixie and Norton back to school with you," her mother had said.

"Actually, I had." Becky opened her suitcase on the bed.

"They're staying here. They'll get better care here. Regular walks, regular meals. Treats. You can't afford to take them to the vet. Can you even afford dog food?"

"Really?" She stopped long enough to give her mother a hard stare.

"I know what we said. But they're happy here." Her mother fidgeted with the hem of her sweater.

"What about Dad?" Becky rested her hands on her hips.

"Dad? It was his idea." Her mother grinned.

And so, the pugs had found a new home. Thoughts of home, memories of conversations with her parents and siblings created an ache in her heart. Even though she'd spent summers either traveling or at camp, Becky had never been homesick. To her, life was an adventure and something wonderful, terrifying, or amazing awaited around every corner.

Now, remembering her family brought pain. For the first time, Becky missed home. She longed to be back with her parents, brothers, and the dogs—and for her mother to be well.

She closed her eyes and pictured Washington Smith, the hero of the great book-to-be, on the big screen. With a smile on her face, she fell asleep.

WHILE SHE DRESSED ON the third morning of Hanukkah, Becky hoped to find another gift on her desk. Guilt at enjoying the one-sided gift-giving warred with gluttonous delight in anticipating another anonymous present. Pushing through the doors of the office building near Hudson Street, Becky felt her heartbeat jump, like the beat of a native drum. Excitement grew in her veins with each floor she passed in the elevator. Finally, the doors opened on seven. Trying not to look anxious, but failing, she brushed past reception with a quick "hello" and made a beeline for her desk.

Yes! There it sat, in all its glory. A small rectangular package wrapped in gold with a blue ribbon.

"Open it," Bridget commanded.

Becky reached for the card taped on top. "From the Hanukkah Elf."

"This is creeping me out," Joy said.

"It's like having a guardian angel," Becky replied. "The Hanukkah Elf." She picked up the gift and shook it. No rattle, so she tore off the paper. A leather-bound volume of her favorite book, *Pride and Prejudice,* its title etched in gold leaf, rested in her hand.

Tears welled in Becky's eyes. "This is my all-time favorite book."

"Anyone could know that. You said it at the Christmas party. Remember? We went around and everyone had to mention their favorite book?" Joy said. "Is it signed?"

Becky opened the volume, bending slightly and sniffing to take in the new-book scent. There was an inscription.

"Yes. It says 'To read over and over. The Hanukkah Elf.' Wow." She smoothed her palm over the cover, enjoying the feel of the soft, supple, expensive leather.

"That cinches it. Only Trevor has the bucks to buy this," Bridget said, then flounced back to her desk.

"Harmon in accounting makes good money. He's single. He could be the one," Joy put in.

"What about Carson Diller in publicity? Didn't you go out with him a couple of times?" Bridget asked.

Becky sucked her lower lip between her teeth, could it be Harmon or Carson? Maybe her Hanukkah Elf was Cody in production? She'd never dated Harmon or Cody, but she had gone to lunch a couple of times and to the movies once with Carson.

"Carson Diller! Carson Diller!" Joy said, jumping up and down.

"Could be," Becky nodded.

Nothing came of her dates with Carson except friendship. Had he changed his mind?

"Do some detective work. I bet you can find out."

Becky smiled at Joy. "We'll see."

"Everyone standing around—not working? Another anonymous gift, Rebecca?" Maryann stood with her hands on her hips. "Come into my office."

"Sorry." Becky shoved the book in her desk and shut the drawer, then followed her boss.

She sat opposite Maryann, across a large glass desk. All the furniture at Homes and Ralph was modern. Stephen Homes explained that books are what's going on now and therefore the publishing offices should look sleek and modern, as well.

"I've sent your evaluation back to you with questions in track changes. Please answer them and return the document to me this afternoon."

"Will do."

"And, tomorrow, flag any places where Gordon's writing needs work, places for the editor to take a longer look."

Becky nodded.

"Here. Read these three and write up evaluations." Maryann tossed three flash drives at Becky.

"When do you want them?"

"When can you have them?"

Becky frowned. She didn't have any plans this week except lighting the candles and licking her wounds. "I guess by the end of the week."

"Good. That's all." Maryann picked up her phone and swiveled in her chair to face the window. Becky got the hint and returned to her desk.

She sighed and opened the email from Maryann. Before she knew it, it was lunchtime.

"Come on, the accounting department is having their holiday lunch and they invited you, me, and Bridget," Joy grabbed Becky's arm.

Becky glanced out the window. There was no precipitation. "What's the temperature?"

"Cold. Who cares? Carson Diller's coming. Your chance to grill him. Come on, Becky, spend a couple of bucks on lunch."

Movement to her right caught her eye. Sam Golden sloughed his coat over broad shoulders and headed for the elevator.

"Okay. You win." Becky opened her drawer and grabbed her purse.

"Good. Interrogate Carson. Find out if he's your secret lover."

Becky held up her palm. "Wait! Whoever this is, it isn't a secret lover."

"Okay, okay, admirer, then."

"Whatever. Let's go." Becky slung her bag on her shoulder and headed for the closet. Just before the elevator doors closed, her gaze connected with Sam's. He smiled and raised his hand. She smiled back. Then he was gone.

Lunch with the accounting department usually meant plenty of drinks and burgers. They didn't disappoint. Wine flowed like water and beer was purchased by the pitcher.

Everyone asked about her mother. How did they know? Word traveled fast at H & R, but within five minutes, they had her laughing at some silly joke.

Joy turned a sharp eye on Carson Diller. "Got all your gift shopping out of the way?"

"Yep. Except my sister. She's a nerd. So hard to buy for," he replied.

"Gift card," Joy said. "buying for anyone special this year? Maybe a Hanukkah present or two or four or eight?"

Carson laughed. "You think I'm Becky's Hanukkah Elf?"

"You could be," Joy said.

"Maybe I am?" He shot a sexy look at Becky. "I hear you're hot to see *The Nutcracker* at Lincoln Center."

"Who wouldn't be?"

"Maybe the Hanukkah Elf has something big up his sleeve." Carson's eyes glowed with mischief.

She felt heat rush to her face. *Is Carson admitting he's giving me those gifts?* Breathless as if someone had punched her in the stomach, she didn't know what to think.

"Guess you'll have to wait and see. Or keep guessing forever," he said, leaning over to whisper the last part directly to Becky.

"Oh my God. What if he doesn't reveal himself? What if I never know who the Hanukkah Elf is?"

"I bet he does. And you might be surprised," Carson said.

"Aha! So you know?" Joy pounced.

"I didn't say that. I'm guessing, just like you." Carson picked up his beer.

Becky chowed down on a Philly cheesesteak. Between the heavy workload and the mystery of the Hanukkah Elf, she'd developed a voracious appetite.

"Another glass of wine?" Carson asked, his eyes gleaming.

Becky shook her head. Could he be the Hanukkah Elf?

THAT NIGHT, BECKY PLACED her new book in her top drawer and stuck candles in the menorah. After reciting the prayer in Hebrew and in English, she gazed out the window. Her room faced the backyard of the townhouse, affording her a view of the rear ends of homes on 93rd Street. Her gaze swept up and down the row houses. Several buildings had picture windows.

She spied families setting up Christmas trees, decorating them, or eating dinner. In some, there were working fireplaces their flames cast a reddish glow. The families had young children, reminding her of when she, David, and Joe were kids, helping to set the table, arguing about who had kitchen duty that night, and anticipating much-desired toys for the holiday.

Sighing, she missed the days of being a child, dependent, and taken care of. Who knew living in New York City on her own would be so stressful? She'd watched reruns of "Sex in the City" over and over, dreaming of living a glamorous life in Manhattan. But reality turned out to be a different picture. Instead of buying exquisite designer clothing, she bargain-shopped, hawking sales. The images of rich dinners in expensive restaurants faded into the mist, replaced by the reality of sharing dishes at the Chinese restaurant. She could barely afford a movie once a month.

Missing her family, Becky wondered if life in the Big City would end up being worth the sacrifices. Had she proven to her father she could make it on her own? Did it matter? Staring out the window, she longed to be part of a family preparing for a celebration. At twenty-eight, maybe she was ready to settle down and start her own?

But she'd need a man—who'd be the right man? Her mind whirled. Would he be the Hanukkah Elf or someone she had yet to meet? Joy and Bridget never tired of endless speculation on the identity of the Hanukkah Elf. Each new suggestion set her imagination in motion. Could she see herself with Harmon from accounting or Carson from publicity? What about Trevor Gorman? Would she give him a chance?

She didn't know any of them well enough to have a valid opinion. And what if he turned out to be someone she didn't like? Perhaps Charlie from the mailroom? No, he'd not have enough money to buy a leather-bound book. Once again, she turned to peep in the windows of her neighbors and imagined herself in those warm, cozy homes, eating the roasts so richly displayed on platters surrounded by potatoes and veggies, and drinking expensive wine poured into gleaming crystal stemware.

She picked up her notebook. Perhaps these windows, the scenes inside, and her dreams would be the inspiration for her first work of fiction? She opened to a fresh, blank page and placed pen to paper.

THE MORNING OF DAY four was frosty and clear. The sun shone a cold light on the sleepy city, just warm enough to melt the remaining snow and ice. Becky bounded out of bed, energized by the story she'd begun the night before, and the promise of a gift on her desk.

She dressed in a plaid skirt, white blouse and red jacket. Festive, she thought as she traipsed through the wet streets to the subway. The hope that the Hanukkah Elf had left something for her spurred her on. She hurried along the sidewalk, not bothering to gawk at the gorgeous Christmas windows of the stores she passed. Hell, she couldn't afford what they were displaying, so why waste time? She arrived twenty minutes early.

When the elevator doors opened, she raised her hand to wave as she skedaddled past the receptionist and headed for her desk. There sat a package, in a horizontal silvery-blue foil bag. It was bigger than before. She tore the card off the gift. *From: The Hanukkah Elf.*

She wished for a more personal message—a hand-written one rather than printed out. Maybe she could identify the handwriting? Shrugging her shoulders, she ripped open one end of the bag and the scent of chocolate met her nose. Her mouth watered.

Becky slid a chocolate babka out. A gentle squeeze revealed it was fresh. Probably purchased that morning. If she could find out who had arrived early...

"Well, hello. I see your secret elf has already made a delivery." Trevor Gorman stood at the other end of her desk, grinning. "Are you going to share?"

"Did you buy this, Trevor?"

"If I said *yes*, would you go out with me?"

"No."

"Then I'm not going to tell you. Share?"

Together they walked to the break room kitchen. Becky fished through the cluttered draw for a knife. Trevor grabbed paper plates from the cabinet. She cut two slices. They sat down to eat.

"This is almost like a date. But cheaper."

"Not funny." Why didn't he get the hint and leave her alone? Was the man's head as thick as a stone wall?

The rich, intense chocolate flavor blended so perfectly with the buttery bread texture. Becky closed her eyes to focus on the deliciously sinful taste experience of the perfect chocolate babka. Damn! The Hanukkah Elf knew where to shop.

"What will it take to get you to change your mind? Flowers every day for a week?"

"Let it alone, Trevor."

"I don't have problems getting other women to go out with me. I'm rich. I'm famous. But none of that seems to mean anything to you."

"I'm not going to end up a notch on your bedpost, okay. Can we leave it there?" She took the last bite of the bread.

"What makes you think I'd get rid of you?"

She made a face and stood up. Damn, the man was ruining her lovely Hanukkah gift.

"I have to get back to work."

"Suit yourself. You don't know what you're missing. And don't be surprised if you get buried with flowers."

She left him alone at the table and hustled back to her desk in time to answer a phone call.

"Becky? Mr. Ralph wants to meet with you at ten."

"Okay."

As she replaced the receiver, her nerves kicked up. Uh-oh. Why did Mr. Ralph want to see her? Had Trevor complained? She swallowed. Mr. Ralph had never summoned her before. She wasn't sure he even knew who she was. Stuck back in her little cubicle, she never even saw him pass by in the morning. What could he possibly want with her? Nothing good.

Chapter Three

She opened her email for the day and tackled an assignment, but her heart wasn't in it. The minute hand on the clock moved slowly toward twelve. Sweat started under her arms and on her forehead. She plucked a tissue from the small box on her desk and smoothed it over her brow.

Jumpy, she headed for the coffeemaker. Not a good idea to pump up on more caffeine, but she simply couldn't sit still or focus on her work. When she picked up the pot, a deep male voice startled her.

"Are you all right?"

Glancing up, her gaze connected with Sam's. "You look pale. Maybe you should sit down."

"I'm okay." Becky stepped back.

"What happened? Is your mother okay?"

"As far as I know. Mr. Ralph wants to see me. I must have done something wrong. Or maybe Trevor complained." She gripped the mug tight to keep her fingers from trembling.

"Maybe it's a good thing?"

"Good? Me? Couldn't be."

"Don't sell yourself short."

Sam poured milk in her brew and offered a packet of sugar. "Take it easy. He's a nice guy."

"If you say so."

He smiled. "Good luck." And returned to his office.

Becky took the coffee, which she didn't want back to her desk and checked her watch. A quick stop in the ladies' room gave her five minutes to refresh her makeup and show up at Mr. Ralph's door on time.

"Come in, come in."

Becky entered and made a beeline for a chair opposite his massive wood desk. Her knees refused to be still.

"Hi, Mr. Ralph. You wanted to see me?" Her voice shook.

"Yes. Relax. I don't bite. Did you write this evaluation of Gordon Albright's book?"

She nodded.

"Maryann was impressed with it."

"Really?" Becky tried to keep the surprise out of her voice but failed.

"She said you're pretty sharp. After reading your evaluation, she read the book and totally agrees with you."

"She does?"

"Don't sound so surprised. It's Maryann's job to spot talent. Since you love this one so much, we thought we'd give you a shot at landing the contract and shepherding the novel through to release. Are you interested?"

Her heart rate doubled. "Do you mean it?"

"Of course. Why do you doubt it?"

"I mean. Well, acquisitions has always been my dream."

"Then you're living proof that dreams do come true. We're having a meeting on January second. I've added your name to the list. Get your thoughts together and be ready to discuss your ideas when we get back."

"I will. Oh, I will, Mr. Ralph. Thank you so much for this opportunity." She stood and shook his hand.

"Don't let me down."

"I won't."

"If you do a good job, there might be a raise in it."

"Oh, thank you for the opportunity." Becky pushed to her feet.

Her feet barely touched the ground as she flew back to her desk. Stopping on the way at Maryann's door, she popped her head in.

"Mr. Ralph gave me the good news. I can't thank you enough for passing along my evaluation."

"It's my job, Rebecca. You spotted a good book. Now we must figure out how to make it great. Glad you're on the team." When Maryann's phone rang, Becky returned to her desk.

Her mind whirled faster and faster, her fingers flew across the keys and could barely keep up with her thoughts.

"Coming to lunch?" Joy asked.

Lost in thought, Becky shook her head and kept typing. At twelve thirty, hunger gnawed at her belly. She stopped, grabbed her sandwich and headed for the cafeteria. Sam sat alone, reading a magazine and munching on lasagna.

Emboldened by his past support, she approached. "Can I join you?"

He smiled and pulled out a chair.

"What happened at your meeting?"

"I can't believe it. You were right."

"You can't believe I was right?"

She sensed heat in her cheeks. "I didn't mean it like that. You were right. It was a good meeting, not a bad one."

Becky summarized it to Sam. While she talked, he worked his way through a huge plate of pasta, nodding at appropriate intervals.

"Confidence, Becky. Maryann tells me you're smart."

"I thought she hated me."

"She can be a little gruff, but don't let that put you off. She's sharp and knows talent when she sees it. She's mentioned you to me."

"She has?"

He nodded. They went on to talk about Gordon Albright's book. Sam shared marketing tips he'd seen used for success. Becky listened.

"Tomorrow's the last day until after Christmas. What do you think the Hanukkah Elf will bring you?" Sam asked.

"I have no idea. Frankly, he's already done more than enough."

"Have you figured out who it is, yet?"

She shook her head. "Carson and Trevor both tease me about it every day. It must be one of them. Unless it's Charlie in the mailroom. Ugh. He's not for me."

Sam laughed. "Do you think he'll reveal himself? If it is a *him*?"

"I hope so. Maybe tomorrow? I'm leaving for Milwaukee on Sunday. At least I'll have the last two nights with my family."

Sam nodded. "Good. I hope your mom is okay by the time you get home."

"That would be the best gift of all."

FRIDAY MORNING, BECKY threw off the covers and bounded out of bed. Would today be the day she'd find out who was the Hanukkah Elf? It was the last day for a present and since the office would be closed for Christmas. Becky needed to be with her family. Unable to get a seat on a plane leaving on Friday night or Saturday, she'd had to opt for a seven-a.m. flight on Sunday.

She slipped on a red velvet dress and black patent leather heels to dress up for the holiday. She tied her hair back in a red ribbon.

All the way to work, she wondered what would be waiting for her on her desk. The Hanukkah Elf had created excitement and anticipation. Anxious at being separated from her family in a time of crisis, Becky had worried every day. The surprise gifts relieved a bit of the tension in her shoulders and put a smile on her face—at least for a while. She looked forward to the new gift and sadness swept over her since it would be the last.

Becky chewed her lip at the thought that maybe the Hanukkah Elf was someone she didn't like or couldn't like or want to go out with. Ugh, how ungrateful to turn her thoughts toward rejecting whoever had been kind enough to help her through a tough time. What would her mother say? She knew the answer. Guilt seeped into her bones. No matter who it was, she had to be gracious and acknowledge the kindness and generosity of the anonymous friend.

She'd risen early and arrived half an hour before the rest of the staff. This gift she wanted to receive alone, privately, not with everyone gawking. When she entered the office, her gaze went straight to her desk. There was nothing there! Her eyes widened and her heart sank. Could he have forgotten? Changed his mind about her? Or been hit by a bus? Instead, there was an envelope.

She hung up her coat, pulled out her chair, took a deep breath, and sat down.

She fingered the envelope with her name on the front. With a shrug of her shoulders, she opened it. Inside was a piece of paper with a printed message and one ticket.

Happy Hanukkah, Becky. If you want to know who I am, come to Lincoln

Center tonight at 7 p.m. to see The Nutcracker. I'll be in the seat next to you. You'll be in a public place and free to leave any time. I hope

you join me. I'm tired of hiding.

The Hanukkah Elf

Sure enough, the ticket had all the ballet information printed on it. And it was for a tier one seat, center section, fifth row. She Googled the seating chart and found hers. Hers was one in from the aisle. She guessed his was the one on the aisle. Her pulse went crazy. She'd always wanted to see that ballet. Her parents had given her the music CD when she was eight and, in three years, she'd worn it out.

How did he know? Relief at finding out who he was without the office crowd around calmed her. Of course, there would be a ton of people, but they wouldn't know them. And it wouldn't be her colleagues, so if the man was hideous, she could hide her reaction well and not have everyone know. But what if he wasn't?

Trevor Gorman and Carson Diller were both good-looking men. Since it was probably one of them, she didn't have to worry about being repulsed. Would she go out with Carson again? If he was the Hanukkah Elf, sure. Why not? What about Trevor? She frowned but conceded she'd give him one date. If he had been showering her with anonymous gifts, how could she refuse him? As for Harmon? Same rule—one date.

Shoving the envelope in her purse, she turned on her computer and opened her email.

"What did you get today?" Joy asked, leaning on Becky's desk.

"Nothing."

"Oh, come on. Nothing? I don't believe you."

"It's private."

"Hmm. A night at his place? Then it's Trevor, for sure."

"Nope." Becky continued to type.

"Well?" Bridget joined them.

"She's not talking. Must have been something spectacular," Joy said.

"A diamond ring, maybe?"

Becky laughed. "No. And stop guessing. I'm not going to tell you."

"Now she shuts down. You're no fun, Cohen." Bridget huffed off to her desk.

Sam Golden sauntered up. "No Hanukkah present?"

"It's personal."

"Personal?" He raised his eyebrows.

"As in, I don't feel like sharing."

"Did he at least tell you who he is? If it's a he?"

She shook her head. "But I'll find out soon enough."

"Oh? How?"

"Oh, no. I'm not telling. Please, Sam, leave it alone."

He raised his palms. "Okay. It's your secret."

"Thank you."

"See you later." He headed for his office. Becky wondered if she'd offended him. They were friends. But she was also friends with Joy and Bridget, and she didn't tell them. Some things a woman wants to keep to herself. And this qualified. If Sam was offended, he'd have to get over it.

His curiosity about today's present snuffed out any tiny hope she'd harbored that he was the Hanukkah Elf. Yes, he was seeing Maryann, yes, he was a manager—she knew all that. But it didn't stop her heart from hoping. If he was the Hanukkah Elf, he wouldn't keep pushing her to tell him what he already knew. He'd probably snicker and slink away.

She sighed. Can't have everything. Now the one thing left on her list was her mother's recovery. Becky had prayed her mom would be home by Monday. She needed to focus on her assignment, so she ignored negative thoughts and focused on work.

BY THREE O'CLOCK, BECKY took her hundredth glance at the clock in the past hour. Talk about time dragging? Joy sashayed around the partition and leaned on Becky's desk. "Okay. So, you're not telling us anything about the Hanukkah Elf now, but after you find out who it is, you'll tell us, right?"

"I don't know."

"You don't know? You'd leave us hanging?"

"Depends on who it is."

"That sucks. We're friends. We've been happy for you to get all that stuff. And you're blowing us off now?" Anger settled in two red spots on Joy's cheeks.

"I don't mean to." Becky put her hand on Joy's arm. "It's just. Well, this is personal now."

"How come?"

"Please don't ask. I'm going to find out who it is tonight. If I can, I'll tell you when I get back after the holiday."

"You're so mysterious."

"I just want to keep this private. Can you understand?"

"It's a little late for that, but I guess, if it were me, I'd probably do the same."

"You're not mad?"

Joy shook her head.

"Good. Thank you."

"Good luck." Joy gave her a hug.

Finally, the clock read five o'clock. People fled as if they were on a sinking ship. Seemed everyone had someplace to go. Becky waited for the second elevator down.

"Happy holiday," Sam said, stepping aside to let her get on first.

"Happy holiday." She made eye contact with him and hid her curiosity. Would he be getting engaged to Maryann over the break? Emotion tightened her throat. Perhaps she'd only get one wish this year, recovery for her mom. That would be enough.

Becky hopped on a crowded subway, barely squeezing in. She got off at 66th Street and walked toward Lincoln Center. The air had been frigid, but at least the wind wasn't blowing.

On a side street, she spied a coffee shop and went in.

The first thing she saw on the menu was soup. Boy, if ever there was a night for soup, this was it. Besides, soup was cheap. She ordered chicken noodle and a small side salad plus hot tea.

While she waited for her food, she took out the ticket and read it over again. Then her phone rang. It was her brother, Joe.

"Hey, glad I caught you before you went out."

"Actually, I'm at a coffee shop. What's up, Joe? How's Mom?"

"I'm calling to tell you they finally found the right antibiotic. She's responding. If she continues to do well, she might come home on Monday."

"Really?"

"Yeah. Honest."

"She'd be home for the last night."

"Exactly. Gotta go. See you Sunday, squirt. Love you."

Emotion tightened in her chest. Tears gathered and spilled down her cheeks. Mom was going to make it. Thank God! Joy and gratitude washed through her.

"You okay, Miss?" the waiter asked.

"Oh, yes. More than okay. My mom's coming home from the hospital!"

"Great." He placed her food on the table.

Happiness bubbled up inside Becky. She inhaled her soup and salad and hit the street. This was the best Hanukkah ever. Mom was going to be okay and now, *The Nutcracker*! She bounced down the avenue, weightless, and grinning.

Sinking into the crowd, she thought she saw a familiar coat, but then it turned out to be worn by a stranger. Tonight, she'd meet the Hanukkah Elf, watch a classic ballet with her favorite music, and Sunday, she'd see her mother. Life was good.

Becky slipped into her seat and struggled her way out of her winter coat. She pulled it up over her shoulders. Directing her gaze to the stage, she was mesmerized by the beautiful curtain and the gorgeous theater. Box seats with red velvet chairs rimmed the sides. The ceiling boasted colorful, intricate artwork. The huge orchestra pit welcomed the myriad of different instruments bringing Tchaikovsky's glorious music to life.

She rummaged through her purse, looking for a lozenge. She liked to suck on them when at the theater, a concert, or ballet. They kept her from coughing and disturbing those around her. She found one and unwrapped it.

The familiar clearing of a throat stopped her. Her heartbeat doubled and her mouth went dry. It couldn't be. Could it? No, no, no way. She turned in her seat to see a handsome smiling face.

"You?"

Chapter Four

"Sam?" Becky barely choked out his name.

"At your service."

"You're the Hanukkah Elf?"

"I am."

"Oh, my God!" Her breath caught in her throat.

The lights went down, and she sat back, still staring at him. He opened his hand and rested it on the arm of the seat. She slid hers into his and he closed his fingers around it. Becky's heart took flight. She swore she'd need a seatbelt to keep from floating to the ceiling.

Sam Golden had been the Hanukkah Elf all along. She should have known. But what about Maryann? She'd have to find out at intermission. The rumors must have been wrong because Sam wouldn't cheat. She leaned closer to him, enjoying the warmth of his large hand and the gentle pressure of his fingers.

The scent of his aftershave wafted toward her. God, he smelled good. The orchestra finished the overture and the curtain went up. They separated hands to applaud but joined them again.

"You're not angry, are you?" he leaned over to whisper.

She shook her head. With his lips so close, she couldn't resist. She turned to him and brushed hers against his.

51

"Get a room. This is the ballet!" Someone behind them hissed.

Sam chuckled quietly and moved back. There was just enough light to see his eyes gleam. He took her hand once again and they nestled into their seats to enjoy the performance.

Becky hit emotional overload and couldn't stop grinning. Imagine, Sam Golden, holding her hand, buying her gifts, and taking her to the ballet. Could this be real?

The pressure from his hand kept her aware of his presence. Tingles shot down her spine and landed in certain places making her shift in her seat. Her jumping pulse destroyed her ability to concentrate on the dancing. She let the music wash over her and her mind wander to where things might go with Sam.

Suddenly the curtain came down—intermission. She turned to face him.

"How about dessert and coffee after?"

"Great. I have so many questions."

"I'm not surprised," he said, chuckling.

"You pulled this off. I never suspected you."

"That was the idea. Of course, I had help from Trevor and Carson."

"What?"

"Yeah. They agreed to do whatever they could to make you think it was them."

She punched his upper arm lightly. "You bum!"

"And it worked. You thought it was them, didn't you?"

"My lips are sealed."

He pushed to his feet and stretched his arms high above his head. "Let's move a little."

She rose next to him but teetered a bit on her heels. Sam took her elbow. "Thanks. I have one question."

"Shoot."

"What about Maryann?"

"What about her?"

"The rumor is you two are about to get engaged."

He laughed. "Never happen."

"But you spend so much time with her."

"We're just friends. She's had a personal problem she needed my help with. I can't discuss it because it's private. But believe me, there's no dating happening."

Becky sighed. Damn, he was free and interested in her.

"I've wanted to ask you out for a long time."

"Why didn't you?"

"You were so focused on work. I didn't think you saw me as anything but a friend."

Now it was her turn to laugh.

"What's funny?" he asked.

"I've had such a crush on you for forever. Oops. Shouldn't admit it, should I?"

He slipped his arm around her shoulders and drew her to him before he bent down to kiss her. His lips were soft and warm against hers. She melted into him, pressing against his chest. Sam tightened his grip on her, holding her fast.

When they broke, the lights flashed. They returned to their seats, resumed holding hands and snuggled closer. After the performance, which got five curtain calls, Sam ushered her outside and down a side street to a little French Café in the West 70s. They took a quiet little table in the corner.

Sam ordered a pot of Earl Grey tea and a plate of assorted pastries. Suddenly hungry, Becky picked up a mini éclair.

"I have to thank you for being my Hanukkah Elf."

He smiled and poured the hot beverage into two cups.

"You saved the holiday, the whole week. I was so upset about my mother..."

"How's she doing?"

"Oh, I forgot to tell you. My brother, Joe, called tonight. Mom's responding to the antibiotic. Looks like she might be home on Monday."

"Great! She'll be there for the last night of Hanukkah."

"Right. I guess Hanukkah isn't totally cancelled."

"Definitely a positive way to look at it." Sam took a sip and selected a small Napoleon. "I never know how to eat these things."

"They're supposed to be messy. I owe you a lot. Your gifts kept my spirits up."

"That was the idea."

She slid her hand over his. "I've never had anybody care about me like that. Except my family."

"You should."

Becky couldn't stop staring into Sam's eyes.

"I have two more Hanukkah gifts for you."

"Really? You've done enough, Sam."

He put his finger over her lips. "I think you'll change your mind when you hear these."

She nodded.

"First, I want to drive you to the airport."

"But my plane leaves at seven in the morning!"

"So we'll leave at four thirty. Won't be any traffic then."

She shook her head. "You're amazing."

"And the second gift is, I want to drive you home when you get back. I'll be in Jersey anyway. You're going in and out of Newark, right?"

"I am."

"I'll drop you at the airport and head to my parent's place. And leave from there to pick you up."

"That is so awesome. You don't have to."

"What will you do if I don't? Take the bus."

"Probably."

"It takes forever."

Becky could hardly believe her ears. "Why me?"

He laughed. "Are you kidding? First, you're the smartest girl in the office. Second, you're the prettiest, too. Did I say you were smart?"

"You did." She sensed a blush stealing into her cheeks.

"You're the nicest girl I've ever gone out with."

"Me? Dirty rat Becky?"

"You're no dirty rat."

"I can be tough."

"So can I. But I'd rather not." He leaned in for a kiss. "How about dinner tomorrow night?"

"I'd love to."

"Great. Pick you up at six?"

"Perfect."

After they finished the pastries, Sam hailed a taxi and took her home. He opened the door and kissed her goodnight, then returned to the cab. Becky floated up to her apartment. She lit the candles in her menorah and said the prayer.

Her roommates had already left for the holiday, so she had the place to herself. She put the song *Sway* on her phone and got undressed. As she peeked out the window at the families across the way preparing for their celebrations, a feeling of warmth stole through her. Soon, she'd be with her family. Then she'd come back to Sam. Who knew where that would go?

Climbing into bed, she uttered a prayer of gratitude. Too excited to sleep, her mind generated a few ideas for Gordon Albright's book. The promotion she'd been busting her hump to get appeared to be within reach. If she focused and worked hard enough, she could turn that dream into a reality.

What about Sam? Was he the one? Their friendship had developed organically over the past year. He had encouraged her not to give up, but put on blinders instead, and work toward her goal. Liking had grown into more in the past few months as their bond deepened. Remembering the touch of his hand sent tingles through her.

Had the time come to take their relationship to the next level? As she pondered her options, exhaustion took over and she was soon asleep.

SATURDAY MORNING, BECKY slept in until eight, then headed for Barnes & Noble to hunt up gifts for her family. There would be two more days to light the lights. Determined to have some celebration with her father and brothers, she bought two presents for each—one real and one gag gift, plus a few for her mother.

Her father be damned. Hanukkah hadn't been cancelled, just postponed, sort of, or shortened. They had two days left to celebrate. She'd hoped her mother would be well enough to join them.

With the afternoon free, Becky folded clothes and packed her suitcase, tucking small, wrapped packages into the valise. Upon closing it, she took a break for a cup of tea. Listening to *The Nutcracker Suite*, she relived her date with Sam. Joy flowed through her as she recalled the feeling of his hand on hers. Sitting close in the cab, he'd kissed her, deeply. Though aroused, Becky had held back, afraid to let her emotions run rampant—still not trusting he reciprocated her feelings. She tingled at the memory.

Her cell jarred her back to the present. It was Sam.

"Hey, I had an idea. About getting to the airport."

"Oh?"

"Don't take this the wrong way, but it might be better if you stayed at my place tonight. I'll sleep on the sofa. I mean if we have to leave at four-thirty, we could catch a little more sleep if we were both in the same place. Know what I mean?"

Becky chewed her lip. *Trust him? Don't trust him? Trust yourself? Don't trust yourself?*

"Beck?"

"Okay. You're right it makes sense."

"So, bring your stuff. I'll pick you up in the car and we can load your suitcase in before dinner."

She smiled at the relief in his voice.

"Great. See you at six."

"Right."

He hung up. Becky put her feet up on the coffee table and cranked up the music. *The Waltz of the Flowers* was playing. Excitement traveled through her body. Spending the night in Sam's apartment created a dilemma. Did she want to sleep with him or not? Of course, she did. But so soon? Would he think less of her? Becky shook her head to banish the old-fashioned notion.

Sam had known her, not well, perhaps, but for a year. It wasn't like he was a stranger. Gradually, lunches with Sam had become more frequent. She recalled the first time they'd shared a table. It had been in March, during the start of a snowstorm. She'd only been at Homes and Ralph for four months.

The falling snow had grown more intense as the thermometer dropped. The cafeteria had been packed with people not willing to brave the miserable weather. Becky had gone down late, about twenty after twelve, holding her little lunch bag. Every seat had been taken, except one.

When she eyed the empty chair opposite Sam Golden, she'd swallowed and decided to return to her cubicle. He'd looked up at her right before she turned toward the door.

"Have a seat," he'd said, as casually as if they had been bosom buddies for years. "Come on. Don't be shy. If you eat at your desk, you'll get crumbs all over your computer." He'd risen and pulled out the chair. Becky had plopped down.

Sam extended his hand. "I'm Sam Golden. Production Manager."

"Becky Cohen. Lowly admin assistant," she'd replied, taking his hand.

His had been warm and strong and much larger than hers. Even then, upon first meeting, his touch had caused a reaction. Once the ice had been broken, Becky's shyness around him melted away. She never missed a bad weather day in the cafeteria. It had almost become an unspoken agreement to meet there if the wind howled or rain flooded the sidewalk.

She sighed. Nope, Sam Golden wasn't an acquaintance, he qualified as a friend. They had discussed everything from politics to growing up Jewish. She'd always wondered if he'd ever ask her out, and now that he had, was she ready? Damn right she was.

She rummaged through her closet and found a bag her parents had bought her to carry her laptop. She unplugged the machine and put it in. Then she fished a satin teddy and matching tap pants from her top drawer. After folding them, she slid them in the bag, along with some toilet articles, a pair of leggings and a long T-shirt to wear on the plane.

She had time for a brief nap, a shower, then dressing for dinner. Sam pulled up in front of the fire hydrant near her building. Becky joined him. He popped the trunk, lifted her luggage inside, and opened the door for her.

Becky slid across the leather seat. Sam drove a silver Rav 4, not a showy sports car, but definitely a man's car. He joined her and put the vehicle in gear.

"We're going to a little French place I like, near the theater district. You like French food?"

"Mais oui, Monsieur." And her father had said studying French wasn't practical. What did he know?

Sam chuckled, shot her a sly grin and replied. "Touché."

"French was one of my favorite classes in college."

"Juniata College, right?"

"You have a good memory."

"In the boonies in Pennsylvania."

"An excellent memory."

"Is that why you came to New York?"

"One of my reasons. It was small. I felt choked. And the publishing industry is here."

"Of course."

He pulled into a parking lot and handed the attendant the key. With a hand on her lower back, he guided her into *Chez Louis*, a small, elegant French Bistro. The walls were a smoky teal blue, the tablecloths cream colored. There was a tiny vase holding two perfect pink roses. The crystal wine glasses gleamed in the soft lighting as did the fleur-de-lis patterned silverware.

Becky translated the menu for Sam. He ordered the wine the waiter recommended—a glass for each.

"If I have to get up at four, I shouldn't drink too much tonight," she said, half to Sam, but more to herself.

He nodded. "You must be excited about going home."

"I am. Mom is coming home Monday morning. I'll have a day to get the house ready."

He quirked an eyebrow.

"Are you kidding? My two brothers and my father have been there for a week on their own. The place is probably a disaster area. That would stress my mom out. She'd run around picking things up and cleaning. Then probably end up back in the hospital."

"You're a good daughter."

"I feel so guilty being here instead of there. Not just missing Hanukkah but not cooking for my dad."

"And your brothers?"

"They share an apartment downtown, but I think they moved back in with Dad after Mom got sick."

"You have a nice family."

"Thanks. I'm lucky."

"Me, too."

The wine arrived and they placed their orders. While they chatted, Sam slipped his hand over hers. Once again, his touch ignited a fire. Becky sublimated her sexual desire into an appetite for food. The waiter brought trout almandine and potatoes au gratin for her and seared hangar steak for Sam.

She dug into her meal as if she hadn't eaten in a week. When she finished, she buttered a piece of French bread, and wolfed that down.

"Are you still hungry?" he asked.

Oh, yes, she was, but not for food. The candlelight sent shadows across the planes of his face. His nose, slightly long was straight, leading to a sensuous mouth. His eyes glowed in the candlelight. Shadow darkened the color of the scruff on his face. While he talked, she studied him. Handsome in an unconventional, masculine way, his looks appealed to her. He dressed well, wearing a navy sports jacket and gray pants. His blue-and-gold striped tie set off his white shirt pressed to perfection. But the best part about Sam was the broad, warm smile. Every time he shined it on her, she melted.

After dinner, they headed to his place. Because the rest of the world was on their way to their holiday destinations already, they found parking on the street in front of his building. He held the door. Expectations kicked up her nerves. When he unlocked the door, anticipation mixed with shyness made her stumble over the threshold. Sam caught her elbow.

"You okay?"

"I didn't drink that much. Just a little nervous, I guess." She collapsed onto the sofa. Sam put her small bag down by the coffee table. "Don't worry. I'm not going to jump you or anything."

"Oh? Too bad. I was looking forward to it." A sly smile graced her lips.

When Sam burst out laughing, the tension evaporated like mist in the August sun. He joined her on the sofa and launched a steamy make-out session. Pushing away, Becky drew a deep breath and glanced at her watch.

"It's eight thirty. If we're going to leave early, maybe we'd better go to bed."

"I thought you'd never ask," Sam said, loosening his tie.

This time it was Becky's turn to laugh. She picked up her bag and disappeared into the bedroom. She undressed and slid the slinky teddy and tap pants on. Then she scooted into the bathroom to wash up.

By the time she came out, Sam had already stripped down to his boxers and was spreading a blanket over the sofa. Becky stood at the archway that separated the living room from the hallway and cleared her throat.

When he turned around, she swallowed, seeing him bare-chested for the first time. Sam had talked about working out on the weekends, but she'd never imagined his body would look quite so buff. His chest appeared firm, partially covered by light brown hair that led from slightly bulging pecs down to his trim waist.

"Holy Hell. Do you actually sleep in that?" he asked.

The heat from his gaze practically melted the skimpy material barely covering her body.

"Sometimes," she squeaked out. She stretched out her arm, her palm facing him. "Come."

A quizzical look shot across his face. "Are you sure?"

She nodded. *Hell, yes, never been more damn sure of anything in my life.*

Two seconds later, he was by her side. "You look awesome. Are you completely sure about this?"

"I am."

"I don't want to rush you."

"We've known each other for a year."

"When you put it that way." He took her in his arms, lowering his mouth to hers. Sam backed them into the bedroom and shut the door with his foot.

Chapter Five

B ecky yawned in the car as it pulled up to the departure section of Newark Airport.

"You didn't get much sleep. Sorry." Sam put the car in park and popped the trunk.

"I'm not. I've never been so happy to be exhausted in my life." She grinned at him.

Sam chuckled as he got out and set her bag on the curb. A representative of the airline took her luggage. She flashed her ID at him and her boarding pass. Sam stood close, his hand resting on her shoulder.

"Please don't rekindle any old relationships in Milwaukee, okay?"

"Don't worry. I won't." She tipped the airline man, and he took her suitcase away.

"Good."

Sam took her hand and led her inside. They approached the security line slowly. Becky hated to say goodbye. Her night with Sam had been a sexy, loving, mutual exploration.

"I've waited a long time. I don't want to lose you now."

"You won't. And don't you find someone else while I'm gone."

He grinned. "There is no one else like you."

Her heart swelled. "It's only a week."

"Yeah. About seven days too long."

Getting up on tiptoe, she whispered in his ear. "I'll count the hours."

Ignoring the early morning crowd, Sam eased her into his embrace for a steamy kiss. When they broke, she ran for the security line, hating to say goodbye. She couldn't resist glancing back. Backing toward the exit, Sam raised his hand in farewell. Becky sighed. Tears wetted her eyes.

"Coming back after the holidays?" a woman asked her.

Too choked up to speak, Becky nodded.

"He'll be here then. It's only a few days."

"But it'll seem like a lifetime," she replied.

The woman patted her on the back. "You're next, honey."

Safely buckled into her seat, Becky closed her eyes, reliving her steamy night with Sam. He'd been passionate and tender. The way he'd kissed her and touched her had ignited a flame that still burned. He had a few years on her, years she guessed he'd spent perfecting his lovemaking. She'd never had a night like that with any other man. Sam had taken control, making sure to arouse her to the point she'd reach satisfaction before he took his pleasure. She could hardly wait for more time between the sheets with her unselfish lover.

A small sigh escaped her lips. Opening her eyes, she looked around to see if anyone had noticed. The older woman sitting in the seat next to her spoke.

"He must be some guy."

Becky felt heat in her face. "He is," she replied. Then shut her eyes again.

As the plane taxied down the runway, Becky remembered resting in Sam's arms, snatching what little sleep they could, snuggled together. Shortly after the aircraft left the ground, she conked out and awoke as the plane began its descent.

Jostled by the hustle and bustle on board as people took down luggage from the overhead racks and jockeyed for position to deplane, Becky's heartbeat quickened. Her family waited for her. Damn, she'd be overjoyed to lay eyes on her pesky older brothers and her father. Her pulse thudded in her ears. She hadn't expected to miss them so much.

As she neared the baggage carousel, she heard a familiar bark or two. There they were, David and Joe with the pugs. Becky ran to them, hugging her brothers as the dogs leaped up, anxiously trying to lick her face. When she'd done with the men, she bent down and snuggled with Trixie and Norton. They slobbered her with wet tongues and much love.

"What color is your suitcase?" David asked.

Within minutes, Becky and the entourage were ensconced in the car, heading for home.

"How's Mom?" she asked.

Her brothers gave her the latest information and assured her their mother was scheduled to return on Monday morning.

"She'll be home for the last night of Hanukkah," Joe said.

"That's great. How's Dad holding up?"

"We'd be glad if you could do the cooking. Dad has a lot to learn," Joe said.

"I've lost five pounds on his meals," David piped up.

"I'm on it." Becky leaned back. With a pug on either side of her, she petted them each in turn. Happiness filled her veins. Her life, previously in the slow lane had ratcheted up to the fast track.

"You guys'll have to give me some work time."

"You brought work home? Oy. Dad's not going to approve."

"But it's the best kind of work. Let me tell you about Gordon Albright's new book."

Becky took over the conversation, bringing her brothers up to date on her almost-promotion and the task she had to complete to get there. She kept information about Sam to herself. Long ago, Becky learned not to divulge anything about any guy she dated to her brothers. They'd tease her incessantly and ask about the guy daily. If she said one negative thing about him, her brothers offered to beat him up.

For the time being, Sam Golden would remain her secret—a delicious secret she'd savor in private.

IT WAS ALMOST NINE a.m. when Becky walked into the house. She unleashed the pups while her brothers carried her luggage up to her room. Her father sat at the kitchen table, finishing a bagel and coffee.

He rose to greet her. Shocked at how thin and pale he was, she hugged him tight.

"I'm so glad you're home," he said, his voice tired.

"Me, too, Dad."

He broke from her. "It was touch-and-go for a while." He returned to his seat and sipped coffee.

Becky refilled his mug and offered some to her brothers. She then filled her own. Together they took up all the seats, except one, at the table. Her father went into details of her mother's illness. From time-to-time, Becky squeezed his hand. When his voice faltered, as it did only twice, her heart broke.

"I'm sorry I wasn't here." Her words were barely audible.

Her father patted her hand. "It's okay. You have your own life. That's the way it should be."

Becky lowered her gaze to her mug.

"Finish up. Your mother's expecting us at noon. We've gotta pick up a corned beef sandwich from Harry's for her."

"Might as well get one for all of us," Joe said.

"Is that a slam on my sandwich making?" Becky's father, Fred, replied.

"Let's be honest. You didn't exactly miss a career at Harry's, Dad," David put in.

With chuckles all around, the family donned their warmest coats and piled into the car. Becky couldn't wait to lay eyes on her beloved mother.

She stood back so the men could enter the room first. Becky leaned against the door jamb and let the shock of how frail her mother appeared sink in. Then their eyes met.

"Becky?" Myra's voice wobbled.

"Mom!" Becky strode in and plopped down on the bed, snuggling her face into her mother's shoulder and burst into tears.

When she stopped, David touched her back.

"Let's eat. Ma's probably starving. I know I am."

Sandwiches and pickles were passed out. The family balanced their food on their laps while Myra Cohen's food sat on the table they moved to her bed.

"I'm coming home tomorrow, Becky. Here's a list of things I want you to do before we celebrate the last night of Hanukkah. Okay?"

"Sure, Mom." She took the piece of paper.

Peppered with questions from her family, Becky answered the ones about work, how she liked New York, her roommates, and colleagues—and managed to skirt any asking about her love life. Not wanting to lie to her family, Becky wasn't ready to discuss anything about Sam. Besides, it was early and there wasn't much to tell—that is, much she could repeat to her family.

After lunch, they returned home. Becky headed to her room for a nap.

"I'll wake you up in time to make dinner," Joe called up the stairs.

"You do that." The dogs followed her upstairs, jumped up on the bed, and cuddled close. She fell asleep with her arms around the pugs, dreaming about Sam.

After her nap, the evening went quickly. She prepared a simple, delicious meal. They lit the lights, saving gift exchange for the last night when Mrs. Cohen would be with them. Becky turned in early.

She said a prayer before going to sleep. Grateful that her mother was alive, she included special words for her. Becky vowed to spend the week cooking up a storm to get her mother's strength back and put the family on an even keel once more.

In the morning, before they headed to the hospital, Becky got a text from Sam.

Can you come back early, for New Year's Eve?

She replied*I'll see if I can change my plane reservation.*
While David drove, Becky used her phone to reschedule her flight back to New York. The rest of the day was lost in transferring their mother to the house, preparing applesauce,

potato latkes, wrapping packages amid general teasing and mayhem.

The warmth of her family's love filled Becky's heart. During dessert, Joe insisted on playing Dreidel with the chocolate chip cookies Becky had baked. Each took a turn at spinning. When the dreidel came up *Gimel* for Becky, she laughed. *Gimel* meant all.

"You keep the cookies," she said, forfeiting her win of the entire pot. "I already have it all."

"I guess Hanukkah isn't cancelled," said her father.

"Just postponed," David said.

"This could actually be my best Hanukkah ever," Becky piped up.

Epilogue

Becky's heartbeat jumped as the plane touched down in New York City. Sam had promised to pick her up. She could hardly stand waiting until it was her turn to deplane. As she hurried to the baggage claim area, a voice called out.

"Becky! Beck!" A hand waving in the air drew her attention.

There was Sam, handsome as ever, his smile warm. She quickened her pace. He scooped her into a tight hug, followed by a hungry kiss.

"Welcome back," he said, his breath warm on her hair.

She cuddled into his embrace, resting her cheek against his jacket as he stroked her back. Suddenly, New York City felt like home.

THE END

Watch for a new series of three Jewish romances, coming in winter 2020.

Keep going for a sneak peek of *Unpredictable Love.*

Books by Jean C. Joachim

ECHOES OF THE HEART
HEATHER & MIKE: THE ONE THAT GOT AWAY
SANDY & RAFE: SECOND PLACE HEART
LIZ & NICK: NO REGRETS
PAIGE & BILL: ONE FINE DAY
ANTHOLOGY
HOCKEY
THE FINAL SLAPSHOT
BOTTOM OF THE NINTH
DAN ALEXANDER, PITCHER
MATT JACKSON, CATCHER
JAKE LAWRENCE, THIRD BASEMAN
NAT OWEN, FIRST BASE
BOBBY HERNANDEZ, SECOND BASE
SKIP QUINCY, SHORT STOP
EXTRA INNINGS
FIRST & TEN SERIES
GRIFF MONTGOMERY, QUARTERBACK
BUDDY CARRUTHERS, WIDE RECEIVER
PETE SEBASTIAN, COACH
DEVON DRAKE, CORNERBACK
SLY "BULLHORN" BRODSKY, OFFENSIVE LINE
AL "TRUNK" MAHONEY, DEFENSIVE LINE

JEAN C. JOACHIM

HARLEY BRENNAN, RUNNING BACK
OVERTIME, THE FINAL TOUCHDOWN
A KING'S CHRISTMAS
THE MANHATTAN DINNER CLUB
RESCUE MY HEART
SEDUCING HIS HEART
SHINE YOUR LOVE ON ME
TO LOVE OR NOT TO LOVE
HOLLYWOOD HEARTS SERIES
IF I LOVED YOU
RED CARPET ROMANCE
MEMORIES OF LOVE
MOVIE LOVERS
LOVE'S LAST CHANCE
LOVERS & LIARS
His Leading Lady (Series Starter)
NOW AND FOREVER SERIES
NOW AND FOREVER 1, A LOVE STORY
NOW AND FOREVER 2, THE BOOK OF DANNY
NOW AND FOREVER 3, BLIND LOVE
NOW AND FOREVER 4, THE RENOVATED HEART
NOW AND FOREVER 5, LOVE'S JOURNEY
NOW AND FOREVER, CALLIE'S STORY (prequel)
MOONLIGHT SERIES
SUNNY DAYS, MOONLIT NIGHTS
APRIL'S KISS IN THE MOONLIGHT
UNDER THE MIDNIGHT MOON
MOONLIGHT & ROSES (prequel)
LOST & FOUND SERIES
LOVE, LOST AND FOUND

DANGEROUS LOVE, LOST AND FOUND
<u>NEW YORK NIGHTS NOVELS</u>
THE MARRIAGE LIST
THE LOVE LIST
THE DATING LIST
<u>PINE GROVE SERIES</u>
UNPREDICTABLE LOVE
BREAK MY HEART
RENOVATING THE BILLIONAIRE
YOU BELONG TO ME
JUST ONE KISS
REWRITE THE STARS
<u>SHORT STORIES</u>
SWEET LOVE REMEMBERED
TUFFER'S CHRISTMAS WISH
THE HOUSE-SITTER'S CHRISTMAS
HANUKKAH'S HEARTS

About the Author

Jean Joachim is an award-winning, USA Today best-selling romance author whose books have hit the Amazon Top 100 list in the U.S. and abroad since 2012. She writes sports romance, small town romance, big city romance, and romantic suspense.

Jean has over 50 books in ebook, print and audio. She writes fulltime, never far from her secret stash of black licorice. An avid bird and dog fan, she has a fondness for chickadees and pugs. A music lover, especially classical, she's married, has two grown sons and lives in New York City. She'd love to hear from you, email her at: sunnydaysbook@gmail.com

Find her books on her website: http://www.jeanjoachimbooks.com

Excerpt from
Unpredictable Love

Chapter One

JORY WALKER PLUCKED three letters from the mailbox in front of the house. Two bills and one envelope addressed to her that looked like it had been through a war. It had, according to what was scratched in the upper corner.

SSGT. T. Stevens

Anger bubbled up inside her. She made a beeline for the house, only to collide with her sister.

"Amber! What the hell?" She waved the envelope in the young woman's face.

"I just sent him one letter."

"This is the fourth you've gotten from him. When are you going to write back?"

"It was a mistake..."

"You can say that again. Especially the part where you signed *my* name!"

"Laura was so convincing. I thought she meant one time. Only one letter."

"She asked people to sign up to write to guys in the military. Not to write only *one* letter and include a lewd photo."

"It wasn't lewd, whatever that means. Just me in a bikini. I'm not good at writing. Much better at pictures." Her beautiful, blonde sister, with a Miss America figure, grinned.

"And the reason you signed my name?"

"I always liked yours better. Besides, if he wanted another letter, I knew you'd write it for me. So, it might as well have your name on it."

"Don't give me that bullshit smile. I'm on to you. And the answer is 'no.'" Jory shoved the envelope from T. Stevens into Amber's hand.

"Please? Pleeeaassseee, Jory. You're the writer. Not me."

"That's right. You're the pretty sister, and I'm the smart one."

Amber nodded. "I don't mean it like that. You're so much better than me."

"Than I."

"See?"

"No."

Amber's jaw jutted out. "Okay. Disappoint some poor guy out there fighting a war. Look at his picture. He's hot, even with a buzz cut. Besides, he might die. Your words could be the last ones he ever sees!"

"He's expecting you, not me."

"Yeah, the picture. But he'll never know. He's in Afghanistan somewhere. Real far away. Just write one or two letters then tell him you got engaged."

"What a mean thing to do! Lead him on then dump him with a lie?"

"You're not going to marry that creep, Archie?"

"Hell, no!"

"Then why do you go out with him?"

"He beats what's on TV. Well, most of what's on TV."

"You deserve better." Amber turned her big blues on her sibling.

As soon as she ramped up the supportive heat, Jory melted. She always did and knew her little sister was manipulating her. But she was powerless to resist. Ever since their parents had been killed in a car crash fifteen years ago, Jory had taken Amber under her wing.

She snatched the envelope from Amber's hand with a snort of disgust and returned to the house. The pretty blonde slid behind the wheel of her car and waved goodbye.

The two girls had had to leave their home in New York City and move in with their widowed aunt, Nan Edwards. It had been traumatic for the much younger one, but Jory had adjusted well. She loved Pine Grove, a small town on Cedar Lake in upstate New York.

Amber was a different story. She dreamt of beauty pageants and Hollywood. New York had given birth to those aspirations, with the promise of fame on every corner, from Broadway to Park Avenue. Pine Grove didn't fit that picture. No one took her seriously, least of all her big sister.

Jory, thirty-two, wrote for the Pine Grove Independent, the town weekly newspaper. It didn't pay much, but spending her days in the company of other newshounds stimulated her curiosity. Then, there was the fun stuff—rubbing elbows with the locals. She interviewed the women's club and covered the softball tournament between the state troopers and the volunteer firemen. She reported the pros and cons of fracking, and kept the community informed.

Respect came her way as an outgrowth of her work. Jory Walker had the ideal job, but it didn't keep her warm at night or send shivers through her in the bedroom.

Amber worked for Beasley's pharmacy, doing makeovers and hawking makeup for the small store. She didn't make much money, but had access to tons of new products, which she tested on herself and her family at every opportunity. She loved her job.

Jory tossed the letter on the kitchen table, in front of her aunt, who sat sipping coffee.

"She's done it again. Damn it," Jory said, pouring her second cup.

Nan glanced at the piece of mail. "Done what?"

"Roped me in." Jory added milk and sugar.

"How?"

"Remember Laura Dailey's drive to get pen pals for military guys in Afghanistan?"

Nan raised her gaze to her niece.

"We wrote about it in the paper."

"Oh, yes. Now I do."

"Amber signed up."

"What's wrong with that?"

"She had no intention of writing more than one letter to this guy, Staff Sergeant T. Stevens."

"That's all? Doesn't seem too serious." Nan shrugged.

"It is when she signs *my* name."

Her aunt sprayed coffee on the table. Her eyes bugged out. "Oh my God! She signed *your* name?" Nan reached for a paper towel.

"Yep. Three letters have arrived from this poor, prolific sap, who's probably wondering why I never answered his first one." Jory shook her head. "The fourth arrived today."

"Maybe he's nice?"

"Good try. I'll answer these then beg off. I'll make up some excuse. Or maybe tell him I have five arms and two heads. I'll think of something." Jory headed for her room and closed the door.

The small, three-bedroom house was tidy and well organized. A large front porch and back deck gave more space for the women to carve out a few minutes of private time. The big backyard, carpeted with a combination of grass and weeds, had been the host of many a kickball game when Amber was younger. Now, it housed an old gas grill and some white vinyl lawn chairs, purchased on sale and looked it.

Jory flopped down on her bed. She had picked up the sturdy, handmade, lavender quilt at a yard sale. The covering echoed her favorite colors, with pink and dark purple flowers against green and white.

She leaned her slim frame back against three pillows and examined the postmarks on each envelope, trying to figure out the order of the letters. She opened the one with the earliest date and pulled out a small photo. Flipping it over, she saw his name neatly printed on the back. Trent Stevens. She smiled at the sexy picture of the Sergeant, stripped to the waist. He wore the short hair of the military, regulation uniform pants, boots, and dog tags, resting against an impressive, if slightly sunburned, chest.

Obviously, he worked out. Her gaze examined the defined pecs, covered with a smatter of dark hair. His biceps were impressive. A hug from SSGT Stevens would be soul-melting. A slight shiver ran through her. *Archie Peabody doesn't look like that.* She hadn't seen all of Archie, since she had refused to sleep with him. But she had seen him in a bathing suit. The words "pasty" and "flabby" came to mind when she recalled images of him at the Fourth of July celebration on the lake.

She sighed. Archie worked at the paper that was owned by his father. They mostly talked shop when they went out. Sometimes, he took her to a movie.

"Archie's better than nothing," she'd said a hundred times to her sister and aunt. But she knew they didn't believe it any more than she did. He was lonely, and so was she. *What's it hurt, having dinner with him?*

She opened Trent's letter. It was a single page, with small, neat script.

> *I gave you all my important intel in my first letter. So this is about other stuff. I like animals. I grew up with a dog and a turtle. Tortoise, really. He was a big guy. Smart, too.*

> *I like American food mostly, but also Mexican. Out here, I'm getting used to MRE's. Basically, I'm a steak and potatoes kind of guy. What's your favorite meal?*

Got to go. Can't talk about where. You understand. Please write soon.

I hope you received my last letter. We live for mail delivery.

Take care,
Trent

Jory took a piece of paper from her writing tablet and grabbed a pen. Before she began, she changed her mind, went to her desk, and pulled out a box of pretty, pink notepaper she had received as a gift but never used. She'd had no one to write a letter to before today. After slipping out a sheet, she leaned on a pad and began.